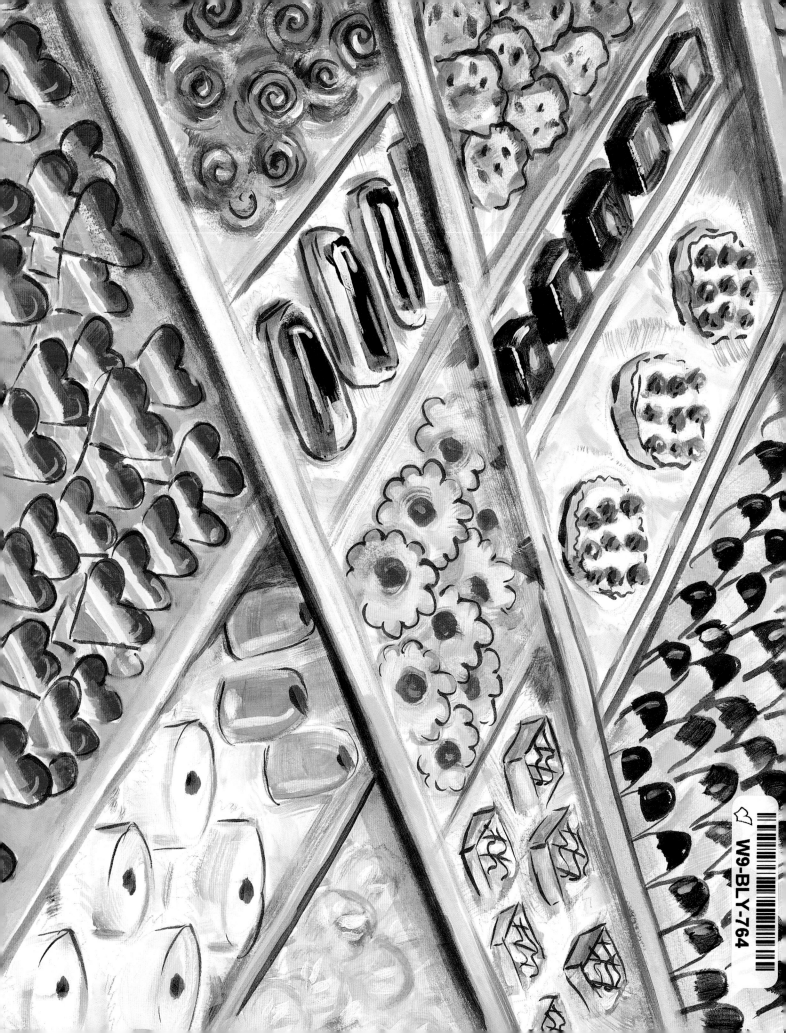

There are no bears in Little Bear Bakery.
I'm the whiskers of this neighborhood.
And if it flutters, scurries, or scampers here,
I know about it.

The name is Muffin.
And this is my tale.

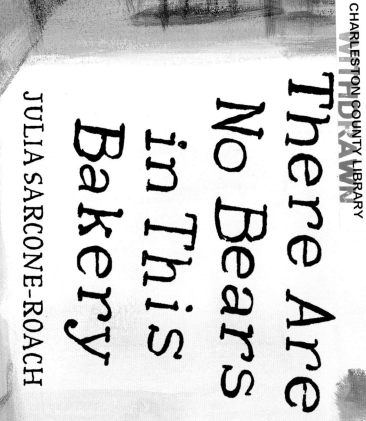

There Are No Bears in This Bakery

JULIA SARCONE-ROACH

Alfred A. Knopf   New York

Each night, the moon rises,
the bread rises, and I rise.

The air cools, and the sounds
get interesting.

That's when the night shift begins.

*Scratch scratch squeak
is the mouse behind
the bakery.*

Clang crash
crunch crunch
is the raccoons
in the dumpster.

Snip snip flap flap aaahhhh!
is the bats visiting the barbershop.

I thought I knew all the night sounds.

Until last night.

Last night, after the sun rolled off the edge of the sky, a mysterious new sound rumbled over the windowsill.

grrrrrrr

I stepped out to investigate.

The air was cool and
wet like a dog's nose.

The alley was empty.

No mouse.

No raccoon.

Not even a bat.

The bakery's back window was open
like a crooked smile.

grrrr

I slipped into the darkness
like icing melting down a hot cake.
Inside, I listened for clues.
Maybe it *was* a mouse.
Mice love sprinkles.

And that is when I saw it.

It was the biggest mouse
I had ever seen.

grrrr

Actually, it was the smallest bear I'd ever seen.

I was surprised.

The bear was surprised.

My tail was the most surprised.

Grrr rumbled from
the bear's belly.

The problem was clear.

Up close, the bear smelled like old socks, cinnamon, and adventure.

And I was on the case.

The rumbling grew softer
and softer until . . .

burp!

For a moment, everything was quiet.
Too quiet.

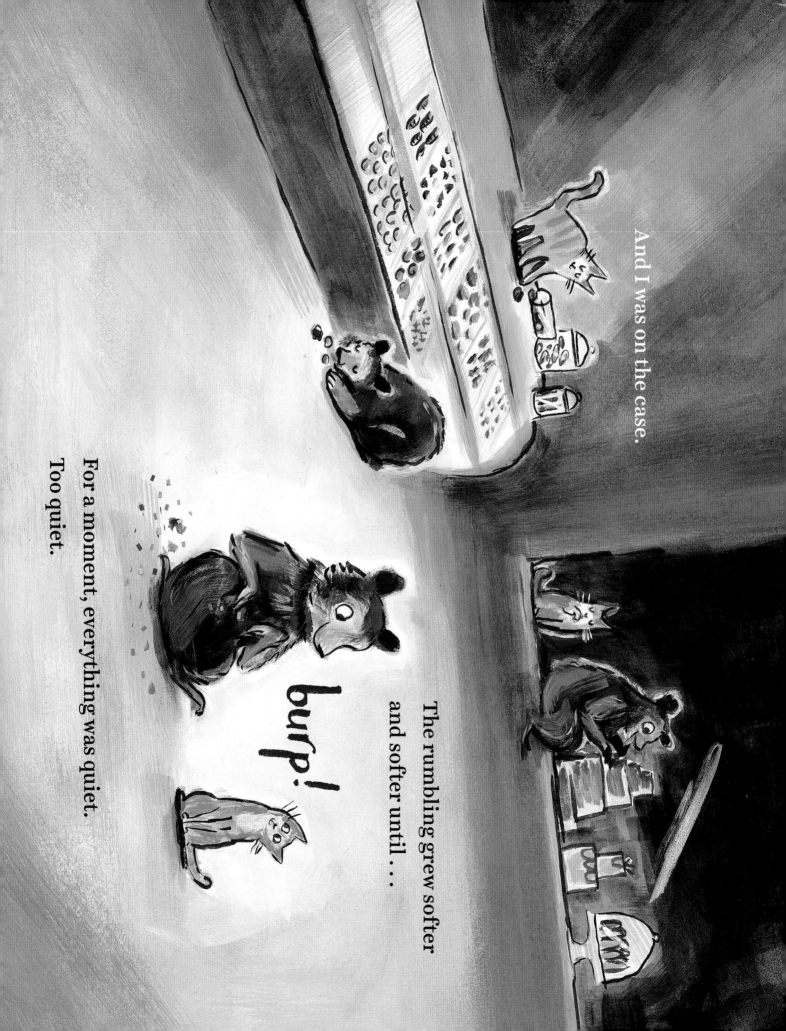

I heard snuffling sounds behind me.
I had a tail.

I mean, my tail had a tail.
I mean, there was something
in the darkness.

The darkness had eyes.

And they were looking at me.

My whiskers trembled.

My paws shook.

It was an enormous bear.

It smelled like the dumpster on a hot day

and rumbled louder than the vacuum cleaner.

Suddenly it was

LIGHTS-OUT!

Everything went dark, and I couldn't move.

I was smooshed, like a muffin between the couch cushions.

I was in the middle of a giant bear hug.

It was warm, like a bath mat in the sunshine.

It smelled like that bath mat needed a bath.

There was a low rumble from somewhere in the fur.

Oh, wait—that was me.

It turns out big bears like sprinkles, too.

Light began to nibble at the edges of the window.
It was time for naps.
Even my shadow was sleepy.
I made sure the bears got on their way safely.

The sun rose and stretched like a yawn down the alley.

The bears rumbled back to the forest.

The night shift had ended.

My job here was done.

purrrrr

So that's it.

Another case closed by Muffin.

No bears in Little Bear Bakery.

Not anymore.

I took care of them.

It was a messy job, but I handled it.

Now it's time for a nap.

By the way, we're out of donuts.

For Yuka and Clotilde

THIS IS A BORZOI BOOK PUBLISHED BY ALFRED A. KNOPF

Copyright © 2019 by Julia Sarcone-Roach

All rights reserved. Published in the United States by Alfred A. Knopf, an imprint of Random House Children's Books, a division of Penguin Random House LLC, New York.

Knopf, Borzoi Books, and the colophon are registered trademarks of Penguin Random House LLC.

Visit us on the Web! rhcbooks.com

Educators and librarians, for a variety of teaching tools, visit us at RHTeachersLibrarians.com

Library of Congress Cataloging-in-Publication Data is available upon request.
ISBN 978-0-399-55665-4 (trade) — ISBN 978-0-399-55666-1 (lib. bdg.)
ISBN 978-0-399-55667-8 (ebook)

The illustrations in this book were created using acrylic paint, cut paper, and marker.

MANUFACTURED IN CHINA

January 2019   10 9 8 7 6 5 4 3 2 1   First Edition

Random House Children's Books supports the First Amendment and celebrates the right to read.